The Mystery of the Attic Lion

THREE COUSINS DETECTIVE CLUB®

The Mystery of the Attic Lion

Elspeth Campbell Murphy
Illustrated by Joe Nordstrom

BETHANY HOUSE PUBLISHERS
MINNEAPOLIS, MINNESOTA 55438

Published by Bethany House Publishers
A Ministry of Bethany Fellowship International
11400 Hampshire Avenue South
Minneapolis, Minnesota 55438
www.bethanyhouse.com

Printed in the United States of America by
Bethany Press International, Minneapolis, Minnesota 55438

Library of Congress Cataloging-in-Publication Data

CIP data applied for

ISBN 0–7642–2135–3   CIP

ELSPETH CAMPBELL MURPHY has been a familiar name in Christian publishing for over twenty years, with more than one hundred books to her credit and sales approaching six million worldwide. She is the author of the bestselling series *David and I Talk to God* and *The Kids From Apple Street Church,* as well as the 1990 Gold Medallion winner *Do You See Me, God?,* and two books of prayer meditations for teachers, *Chalkdust* and *Recess.* A graduate of Trinity College and Moody Bible Institute, Elspeth and her husband, Mike, make their home in Chicago, where she writes full time.

Contents

"Then wolves will live in peace with lambs. And leopards will lie down to rest with goats. Calves, lions and young bulls will eat together. And a little child will lead them. Cows and bears will eat together in peace. Their young will lie down together. Lions will eat hay as oxen do. A baby will be able to play near a cobra's hole. A child will be able to put his hand into the nest of a poisonous snake. They will not hurt or destroy each other on all my holy mountain. The earth will be full of the knowledge of the Lord, as the sea is full of water."

Isaiah 11:6–9

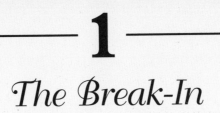

1

The Break-In

"*T*hat's the odd part," said Titus McKay's grandaunt Barbara. "Not a single thing was taken."

"And you're sure about that?" asked Titus's father again.

"Not that we can tell, anyway," said Granduncle Frank. "The television. The VCR. They're still here. Barbara has some nice pieces of antique jewelry and old family silver. None of that is missing. My stamp collection wasn't even touched."

Titus's mother gave a worried frown. "It doesn't make sense. Why would anyone break into a house and not take anything?"

No one had an answer for that. They had gone over and over it already—the way people do when something upsetting has happened.

Frank and Barbara Titus were like Titus's grandparents on his father's side. Titus's real grandparents had died years before Titus was even born. Titus's father, Richard, had gone to live with his aunt and uncle when he was a teenager. He loved them like his own parents.

So when Titus was born, he got the Tituses' *last* name for his *first* name.

Needless to say, Granduncle Frank and Grandaunt Barbara thought Titus was the most wonderful child in the whole history of the world.

Titus and his parents lived in a high-rise apartment building in the city. Frank and Barbara also lived in the city. But they had an old house in a quiet old neighborhood. Nothing like this had ever happened to them before.

When Titus and his parents got the call about the break-in, they came right over.

Titus's cousins (on his mother's side) were visiting, so they came along, too. Timothy Dawson and Sarah-Jane Cooper knew Frank and Barbara Titus from visiting before. In fact, the last time Timothy and Sarah-Jane were there, the three cousins had solved a "doggy" mystery.

(The three cousins had a detective club, and solving mysteries was something they loved to do.)

Titus wished someone could solve this one, but the police had not sounded very hopeful.

Suddenly he thought of something important.

"Did you check the attic?" he asked.

2

The Den

*G*randaunt Barbara looked at Titus in surprise. "No, sweetie, I'm sorry. I never even thought to check the attic. These old knees don't like to climb up there any more than they have to. You don't keep anything valuable up there, do you?"

"No," said Titus. He shrugged, trying to look casual about it. But the attic was his special place.

Ever since he was little, Titus loved to climb. And he loved being up high. So his granduncle Frank had built him a tree house in the backyard and a playroom in the attic. When the weather was warm, Titus spent most of the time in his tree house. Now that the weather had turned cold, he was spending more time in the attic.

In all the excitement, he and his cousins hadn't been up there yet today.

Frank and Barbara seemed to understand that Titus was nervous about his stuff.

"Go check," said Granduncle Frank.

"Good idea," said Timothy.

"We'll come with you," said Sarah-Jane. "It doesn't hurt to check—even though the burglar probably didn't get that far."

She paused. Sarah-Jane loved words and was kind of particular about them. She said, "I guess we can't really call him the *burglar* if the house wasn't burgled. We could call him the *intruder,* maybe."

That wasn't much better, Titus thought. Even if it turned out none of his stuff was missing, he still couldn't stand the idea of anyone intruding into his space. It made him suddenly realize how bad Granduncle Frank and Grandaunt Barbara must feel. This was their *home.*

Titus wasn't much of a hugger, but he stopped to give them both a quick hug on his way upstairs.

He was glad to be checking the attic. It made him feel that he was somehow *doing* something about all this.

The three detective cousins climbed the stairs to the upstairs hallway.

Tucked away at the end of the hallway was a storage closet.

Inside the closet was a rack jammed full of off-season clothes.

Behind the clothes was a tiny door.

Behind the door was a narrow flight of stairs, leading steeply up.

At the top of the stairs was yet another door.

Titus opened it and switched on the lights. The three cousins stepped into a wonderful room. It was full of books and toys and various projects Titus was working on. There was even a CD player and a little TV set.

Titus's room at home was borderline messy. But, for some reason, he kept his attic playroom—he now called it his den—as neat as a pin. He was even kind of persnickety about it.

So he knew immediately that something was wrong.

"Everything looks fine, Ti," said Timothy.

"Yes," agreed Sarah-Jane. "The den looks great. Nothing's missing, right?"

"I don't think so," said Titus. "But I'll tell you one thing. Someone has been here."

3

The Lion in the Attic

*T*itus's cousins looked at him in surprise.

"How can you tell someone has been here?" asked Timothy.

Titus looked around. How *could* he tell? Little things were just "off" somehow.

A pencil on the floor that he knew he had left on the desk.

Throw pillows on the window seat that he knew were "out of order."

A door at the back of the room left slightly open that he knew he had closed.

He explained all this to his cousins.

"What do you think it means, Ti?" asked Sarah-Jane.

Titus looked around, trying to "read" the clues. He said, "Well, maybe the intruder thought he heard a car drive up or something, so he went to the window to look out. Maybe he knocked over the cushions and put them back in the wrong place.

"Then maybe he left in a hurry and knocked the pencil to the floor without noticing it.

"But the most important thing is that door. He must have looked to see what was back there."

Titus's den took up only part of the attic, and it was the only part that was heated. So the back door was always kept closed.

The rest of the attic was used for storage.

An old attic can be filled with lots of interesting things. Titus had explored every nook and cranny of this one. He loved crawling into tight spots and digging through old trunks.

The most fascinating thing he had found was a lion.

Not a real live lion, of course. (Although Titus had liked to pretend it was real when he was little.)

It was a beautifully carved statue of a sleeping lion tucked away back in a dark corner. Titus had found it years ago, and it had always

been one of his favorite things. It was too heavy for him to haul out, so he had just left it there. He had named the lion Alexander.

Even now, Titus always made a point of going back to dust off his friend and say hello.

The cousins stared nervously at the half-open door.

They had been back there millions of times, but today it felt a little spooky.

"I guess we'd better check," said Titus.

"I guess so," said Timothy.

"I guess so," said Sarah-Jane.

Titus marched over to the door and boldly pulled it all the way open. Then he stepped through and tugged on the string for the overhead light.

As soon as the light came on, the cousins felt a lot better. Everything looked so ordinary. Nothing seemed to be disturbed.

Except the dust on the floor.

"Footprints," gasped Sarah-Jane.

"Big footprints," said Timothy.

"Not our footprints," said Titus.

Carefully they followed the footprints as they led past the old trunks. Past the broken furniture. Past the boxes of this and that.

"We have to stop and say hello to Alexander," said Titus as the footprints neared his corner.

But it was there that the footprints stopped.

And Alexander was gone.

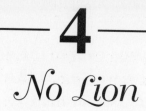

No Lion

The three cousins burst breathlessly into the kitchen.

"No lion!" gasped Titus.

The adults looked up in confusion.

"No lyin'," repeated Granduncle Frank. "No lying about what?"

"No, no, no!" exclaimed Titus. "No *lion*!" This didn't help any.

"What lion?" asked Grandaunt Barbara.

Now it was Titus's turn to feel confused. "You know—*the* lion! The lion in the attic. *Alexander!* He's been there forever. And now he's gone!"

There was a long pause. Everyone looked at everyone else in complete bewilderment.

Suddenly Granduncle Frank laughed and

said, "Oh, *that* lion! You haven't mentioned Alexander in a long time, Titus."

"Oh, right!" exclaimed Grandaunt Barbara. "It was just the cutest thing! Titus used to talk about Alexander the lion all the time. I'm sure we must have told you about it."

"Of course!" said Titus's mother. "I remember now."

"Imagination is a wonderful thing," said Titus's father proudly. "I remember when—"

Titus held up his hand. "Wait a minute!" he cried. He knew it wasn't polite to interrupt. But he was beginning to realize something crazy, and he couldn't quite believe it.

"Let me get this straight," said Titus slowly. "You don't mean to tell me . . . that all this time . . . you guys thought . . . that Alexander . . . was *IMAGINARY*?"

His father looked at him in amazement. "Well . . . *wasn't* he?"

"NO!" cried Titus. "No, no, no!" He turned to his cousins, who were staring at the grown-ups in disbelief.

The adults stared back, also in disbelief.

"You mean . . ." said Grandaunt Barbara slowly. "There really *is* a lion in our attic?"

21

"Yes!" cried Sarah-Jane. "Well, not a real *live* lion, of course. That would be crazy."

"Just what kind of lion are we talking about?" asked Granduncle Frank. "I mean, what does he look like?"

"He's made out of some kind of metal," said Titus.

He turned to Timothy, who knew a lot about art.

"Bronze, I think," said Timothy.

"Alexander is *so* beautiful!" said Sarah-Jane. "Very dignified. Not the least bit scary. He's lying down, sound asleep. He looks so peaceful! But Grandaunt Barbara, Granduncle Frank, how come you didn't know about Alexander if he's in your attic?"

Grandaunt Barbara shook her head. "I can't imagine! This is the first I'm hearing about him, and we've lived here a long time. Whereabouts in the attic did you find him?"

"Come see," said Titus. "Come see!"

5

A Picture of Alexander

The cousins led the adults up to the attic, and everyone crowded together in Titus's little den.

It took a while—quite a while—to explain about the clues of the mixed-up cushions, the dropped pencil, and the half-open door.

Finally, everyone trooped through the door to see the spot where Alexander had been.

Titus made them all step around the footprints. The footprints weren't very clear—more like big smudges on the floor. They probably wouldn't help anyone track down the burglar. But at least they showed the grown-ups that the cousins weren't totally out of their minds. Somebody really *had* been up in the attic.

"There!" said Titus, pointing to a cramped little corner. "That's where Alexander was. See? You can tell by the mark on the floor."

Everyone looked. Sure enough, there was a clean spot on the dusty floor. It showed that something had been there recently that wasn't there now.

For a moment, everyone just stood looking at the spot where the mysterious lion had been.

Then Titus's father said, "At least you kids know what this lion looks like. We don't even know that."

Suddenly Timothy had an idea. "I could draw you a picture of Alexander," he said.

"Great idea!" cried Sarah-Jane and Titus together.

Timothy was *extremely* good at art. Kids at school were always asking him to draw pictures for them.

So everyone went back to the den.

Titus picked up the pencil, got out some paper, and sat Timothy down at the desk.

Timothy sat hunched forward with one arm curved around the paper.

"Honestly, Tim!" muttered Sarah-Jane.

"It's not like we're trying to copy off your test paper or anything."

But she and Titus got the message. Hard as it was, they had to step back and let Timothy work. They knew how annoying it was to have someone standing over your shoulder when you were trying to concentrate.

And, of course, Timothy *did* have to concentrate. After all, he didn't know Alexander nearly as well as Titus did.

Timothy closed his eyes, trying to picture

Alexander in his mind's eye before he began to draw him.

After what seemed like a *very* long time, Timothy began to draw.

By this time, Titus and Sarah-Jane were almost bouncing up and down with impatience.

"Hold your horses," said Timothy calmly, without even looking up. "This will just take a minute."

It took a lot longer than a minute. A lot of sketching. A lot of erasing. But at last Timothy announced, "Finished!"

Titus and Sarah-Jane rushed over to inspect the picture before they showed it to the adults.

It was just as they had expected.

"EX-cellent!" declared Titus. "It looks *exactly* like Alexander!"

"So cool!" agreed Sarah-Jane. "It's an *extremely* good drawing, Tim."

Titus held the picture up for the grown-ups to see. He said, "This is Alexander, the Attic Lion."

Everyone agreed that it was a beautiful drawing of a beautiful lion.

All except Titus's father.

He stared at the drawing as if he couldn't quite believe what he was seeing.

At last, he said, "I *know* this lion."

6

No Ordinary Lion

The cousins looked at one another in surprise. This was the last thing in the world they expected to hear. The day had started out confusing and was getting more confusing by the minute.

"This is no ordinary lion," murmured Titus's father.

Titus had never thought Alexander was the least bit ordinary. But things still weren't making sense.

Titus said, "Dad! You didn't know Alexander even existed until a little while ago. You thought he was *imaginary*. So how could you know him?"

"I've seen a picture of him," replied his father.

Timothy said what Titus was thinking. "How could you have seen a picture of him, Uncle Richard? He's been tucked away in the attic for years and years. Are you saying someone sneaked up here and drew a picture of him? Who? Why?"

"No, it wasn't a drawing," replied Titus's father. "It was a photograph. A very old photograph. And it wasn't taken in the attic. It was taken when Alexander was out in the world."

" 'Out in the world'?" repeated Sarah-Jane. "What does that mean?"

"It means that Alexander may have been tucked away in this attic for years and years. But if he's the same lion I'm thinking about, he's also been missing for years and years."

"Missing!" cried Grandaunt Barbara. "From where?"

"From the old library on Montgomery," replied her nephew. "Alexander was one piece of a sculpture that was attached to the wall by the front door."

Granduncle Frank frowned. "There is no library on Montgomery. Hasn't been for years."

Titus's father nodded. "My point exactly."

"Dad . . ." began Titus.

His father laughed. "I know. I know. Get to the point. Right?"

Titus's father was a college professor, and sometimes it took him a while to explain something because he liked his students to ask questions.

"OK," he said. "Here it is. For a long time now, the city has commissioned art for its public spaces. That means they hire an artist to do a painting or a sculpture to decorate a park or a building. In this case, the artist was the famous sculptor Augustus Finch.

"Unfortunately, the city hasn't always done a good job of keeping track of this valuable art. When a building is torn down, for example, sometimes the art gets lost in the rubble or gets stashed away somewhere. A friend of mine at the university—Lois—is on a committee that's trying to find lost art. That's how I happened to see the photograph."

Titus was trying to remember something his father had just said. Something he needed to ask about . . .

"Did you say Alexander was one *piece* of a sculpture?"

"Yes," said his father. "One of two pieces. See how the lion's body is curved here?"

"Yes," said Titus. "I always thought it looked as if something was missing."

"Well, you were right," said his father. "Alexander is supposed to be cuddled up to a lamb."

7

The Peaceable Kingdom

"*A* lamb!" cried Sarah-Jane. "You mean the lamb is lost, too? Oh, the poor little thing!"

"S-J!" groaned Timothy. "It's not a *real* lamb. It's a *sculpture* of a lamb. Besides, it seems that the lamb would be in a much worse fix if it was cuddled up next to a lion."

Sarah-Jane heaved an exasperated sigh. "Honestly, Tim! How could the lion hurt it? It's not a *real* lion. It's a *sculpture* of a lion."

"Alexander wouldn't hurt anyone!" declared Titus.

Then he paused. He and his cousins did not always have meaningful conversations. In fact, some of their arguments were downright silly when you stopped to think about it.

He said (seriously this time), "A lion and a

lamb *don't* seem to go together, though. I mean, in real life, some animals hunt other animals for food. If a lion was by the lamb, he would probably eat it. If a lamb was by the lion, he would try to run away. They wouldn't curl up together and take a nap!"

"That's exactly the point of the sculpture," said his father. "A lion and a lamb *don't* go together naturally.

"But the idea of all sorts of animals gathered safely together is from the book of Isaiah in the Bible. It's a prophecy about the Messiah's coming and a time of such peace that even the animals will get along.

"Wolves and lambs. Leopards and goats. Lions and calves. Bears and cows. It's called *The Peaceable Kingdom.*"

He looked mischievously at Sarah-Jane. "It even says that a baby can play with a cobra and not get hurt."

Sarah-Jane shuddered. So did her aunt. They both *positively hated* snakes.

And in Sarah-Jane's opinion, cobras were particularly nasty.

"So anyway," continued her uncle. "You often see paintings of all these animals in a group, with a little child leading them. But sometimes the other animals are left out and you just see a lion and a lamb. A lion and a lamb sitting together is a symbol of peace."

"Not a bad sculpture for a peaceful place like a library!" said Titus's mother, who was a librarian herself.

Timothy said, "Uncle Richard's friend is going to be so excited when she hears that we found the lost library lion."

"Yes!" agreed Sarah-Jane. "Tim's drawing proves it. You should definitely show her Tim's drawing, Uncle Richard!"

"Uh . . . guys," said Titus. "Aren't we forgetting something? Sure, Alexander is probably the lost library lion. But the fact is he's *still* lost. Or . . . at least, lost *again*. First he was gone from the library. And now he's gone from the attic."

Titus paused and said more to himself than the others, "And, you know, that's the funny thing."

8

Very Weird

"*F*unny ha-ha or funny weird?" asked Sarah-Jane.

"Funny weird," said Titus.

"What's funny weird?" asked Timothy.

"How did the burglar know where the lion was?" asked Titus.

Everyone looked at him in surprise.

"Think about it," said Titus. "What kind of burglar walks past a TV and a VCR to check out the attic?"

It took a moment for this to sink in.

Timothy said, "And how did the burglar even know how to get up to the attic in the first place? Because—even if you looked in the up-stairs hall closet—that's all you'd think it was. A closet full of clothes."

Sarah-Jane nodded. "Unless you pushed the clothes aside, you wouldn't have any idea that there was an attic door there at all."

Titus's father said, "Yet the burglar walked right through the house. Went straight up to the attic. And didn't take a thing. Except Alexander."

Titus's mother said, "He didn't even have to tear up the attic looking for him. He seemed to know right where he'd be."

"Right," said Titus. "Don't you think that's weird?"

Everyone agreed that it was weird.

Very, very weird.

9

The T.C.D.C.

They were all quiet for a moment, thinking about this.

Then Grandaunt Barbara said, "We should let the police know that something is missing from the break-in after all."

"Good idea," said her nephew.

"And," said Titus's mother. "Maybe we should let Lois know that we found the library lion. Sort of found him, anyway."

Timothy's father nodded. "I'll call her. It would help if I could fax her Timothy's drawing, too."

Granduncle Frank and Grandaunt Barbara didn't have a fax machine. But there was one at a little drugstore down the street.

The police station was also not too far away.

"Well," said Granduncle Frank. "I don't mind taking care of those things. Do me good to get out for a little walk. Anyone want to come along?"

"Me!" cried Titus.

"Me, too!" cried Sarah-Jane.

"Me, three!" cried Timothy.

So everyone came down from the attic, and the cousins ran to get their coats. It felt good to be *doing* something about Alexander.

Titus's father got Lois's fax number from her and dictated it to Timothy, who printed it carefully on a slip of paper.

On the way downstairs, the cousins had decided that Timothy should be the one to fax the drawing. Yes, the attic—and Alexander—sort of belonged to Titus. But Timothy was the one who had made the actual picture.

Being a cousin meant making lots of decisions like this.

They stopped at the drugstore first. Timothy gave the drawing to the clerk. After the fax went through, the clerk gave the drawing back to Timothy.

Then it was on to the police station. On the way, the cousins decided that maybe it would be best if Granduncle Frank did the talking.

Fortunately, they got the same officer who had come to the house that morning.

Even so, it took a while—quite a while—to explain that there was something missing from the break-in after all. Something that didn't belong to the Tituses. Something the Tituses didn't even know they had.

"Can you describe this lion?" the officer asked.

"We can do better than that," said Granduncle Frank. "We can show you a picture of him. Thanks to the T.C.D.C."

"What's a 'teesy-deesy'?" asked the officer.

"It's letters," explained Sarah-Jane. "Capital T. Capital C. Capital D. Capital C. It stands for the Three Cousins Detective Club."

"Detectives, eh?" said the officer. "Well, keep up the good work."

Timothy gave Titus the drawing to give to the police officer. After all, the attic and Alexander *did* sort of belong to Titus.

The officer made a photocopy of the drawing to add to his report. He handed the origi-

nal to Titus, who gave it back to Timothy.

Then everybody said thank you very much, and the cousins and Granduncle Frank left for home.

"Well, it's good to get those things taken care of," said Granduncle Frank.

The cousins agreed.

But it was also kind of a letdown. The exciting feeling of *doing* something was gone.

Three detective cousins looked at one another.

They were all thinking the same thing.

Now what?

10

Questions

*G*randuncle Frank went in the house. But the cousins just wanted to think some more and talk things over. So even though it was a little too cold for it, they climbed up to the tree house.

Then they settled down in a circle and took turns asking questions.

It was a kind of game they had started playing to solve mysteries.

The first rule was that there was no such thing as a dumb question. In other words, you couldn't make fun of another cousin's question.

The second rule was that you had to try not to ask dumb questions. In other words, you had to be serious. Coming up with good ques-

tions was a way of getting your brain fired up.
And asking the right questions could be just as
important—and just as hard—as coming up
with the answers.

The third rule was that it was OK not to
have all the answers. Or even *any* answers.

The important thing was to be honest
about what you really wanted to know. And
then you could trust that the answers would
come along in their own good time.

So the cousins sat in a circle and took turns
coming up with good questions.

This time they decided to go alphabetically, so Sarah-Jane started. "OK. What I really want to know is: What happened to the lamb?"

Another rule said you could ask a "piggyback" question if it had something to do with your first question. So Sarah-Jane said, "Piggyback: How did the lamb and the lion get separated if they're supposed to be together?"

Timothy came next. "What I really want to know is: Who broke into the house and took Alexander?"

Titus said, "I'll ask the same question I asked before when we were up in the attic: How did the thief know exactly where to look? And piggyback: Who would know how to get up in the attic?"

It was Sarah-Jane's turn to ask her next question. But another rule said that if you had a possible answer, it was OK to take cuts and say it. (Even if your answer sounded like more questions.)

Timothy said, "Answer: How about the people who lived here before Grandaunt Barbara and Granduncle Frank? They would know how to get up in the attic. Right?"

Titus and Sarah-Jane nodded.

Sarah-Jane took her next turn. "Has Alexander been in the attic ever since the last people lived here?"

Timothy said, "If Alexander has been there all this time, why did someone take him *now*—and not a long time ago?"

It was Titus's turn. "What's that?" he asked.

11

Bird's-Eye View

Sarah-Jane and Timothy looked at Titus in surprise. It wasn't a dumb question, but it didn't exactly make sense, either.

"What's what?" asked Timothy.

(It wasn't his turn to ask a question, but Sarah-Jane didn't mind.)

"Those marks down there in the yard," said Titus, pointing.

The cousins hadn't noticed the marks before when they were down on the ground themselves. But now they had a bird's-eye view. The marks were two faint straight lines, parallel to each other. They started just outside the back door. If you looked very hard, you could trace them across the yard to the place where they disappeared into the alley.

Sarah-Jane said thoughtfully, "It looks like a dolly made those tracks."

"A *dolly*!" cried Timothy.

"S-J!" said Titus. "This is no time for stories. Certainly not stories about *dolls*!"

Sarah-Jane stared at them. "What in the world are you two talking about?" she asked.

"What are *you* talking about?" asked Titus. "Your doll collection, right?"

Sarah-Jane groaned and rolled her eyes so high Titus thought they were going to pop right out of her head.

"I didn't mean a *doll*-dolly," she cried. "How old do you think I am? Three? I meant a *dolly*-dolly!"

Timothy and Titus glanced at each other. They knew Sarah-Jane was saying something important, but they didn't know what it was.

"A *dolly*!" cried Sarah-Jane again. "You know—it's like a little platform on castors. Ball wheels. It looks like a flat wagon."

Sarah-Jane's father was a builder, and she knew about these things.

"Oh, a *dolly*!" said Timothy and Titus together.

"Yes," said Sarah-Jane. "A dolly. You use it

for pulling something heavy. . . ."

The cousins looked at one another. Without another word they scrambled down the tree and rushed over to the dolly tracks.

12

Dolly Tracks

Now that they knew the tracks were there, the cousins were able to see them on the ground. They traced them from the back door, across the grass, to the spot where the gate opened onto the alley.

That was when things got tricky. The alley was paved. No grass to show tracks.

The cousins stood for a moment, wondering what to do next.

They were pretty sure that the dolly had been used to carry Alexander the lion away.

But they couldn't tell which way the dolly had gone.

Up and down the alley they could see patches of mud or dirt. It was just possible the dolly had passed through those patches and that they could pick up the tracks.

"Well," said Titus. "We've got only two choices here. Right or left. That means whichever one we pick, we have a fifty-fifty chance of being right. I mean, correct. Of course, we also have a fifty-fifty chance of being wrong."

Timothy shrugged. "So it's no big deal. If we pick the wrong direction, we'll just start over."

"Right," said Sarah-Jane. "I mean, true."

But since Sarah-Jane had just said the word *right*, they decided to turn to the right.

They walked slowly down the alley, turning their sharp detective eyes to the ground. (They also had to watch out for cars. But fortunately no cars came along just then.)

They studied every little patch of dirt. Every little bit of grass along the edge.

It was picky work.

Even a little boring.

And they came up with nothing.

The cousins weren't too upset by this. Solving mysteries was fun, but that didn't mean it was easy. And they knew that something could be hard work and fun at the same time.

By the time they came to the cross street, they were almost positive that they had turned the wrong way.

So they retraced their steps to the Tituses' back gate.

This time they turned left.

Again they examined any little patch of dirt or mud for dolly tracks.

They hadn't gone very far when Titus suddenly cried, *"Eureka!"*

This was a fancy word that meant "I have found it." It came in handy for those times when you made an important discovery.

Timothy and Sarah-Jane came rushing over.

Sure enough, there were marks that could only be dolly tracks in a little patch of dirt. And *those* tracks meant that the *cousins* were on the right track.

They continued up the alley, finding traces of the dolly here and there.

It had come this way, all right.

But how far?

Suddenly there was a spot where the tracks turned off the alley.

And stopped at a garage.

The door was closed.

The windows were high up.

And there didn't seem to be anyone around.

The cousins looked at one another.

Was Alexander in there?

13

A Peek in the Window

*T*he cousins knew better than to go barging into a strange building.

Still, they were positively *dying* of curiosity.

They looked up at the high windows. If only they had something . . .

They looked around.

Some loose cinder blocks lay on the ground nearby.

"What if we piled those up?" whispered Timothy.

(Without even having to talk it over, the cousins knew it was best to keep their voices down.)

"That could work," replied Titus softly.

The stand they made was a little rocky. But Titus was good at climbing. He figured he could probably keep his balance. And he wouldn't have far to fall anyway. It wasn't like falling out of a tree or anything. He had done that once in his life, and he didn't plan to do it again.

Titus grabbed Timothy's shoulder for balance and took a giant step up.

Once he was on top of the blocks, he could hold on to the window ledge for support.

He stood on tiptoe and peeked in the window.

What he saw made him give a little gasp.

"Well?" squeaked Sarah-Jane. It was *very* hard to speak quietly. "Well? Well?"

"There really is a dolly!" said Titus in amazement.

Even after all that tracking, he could hardly believe that they had been right.

"Is Alexander on it?" asked Timothy.

"Something is," replied Titus. "But I can't tell if it's Alexander or not. It's covered with a big piece of burlap."

Titus peered farther into the garage and gasped again.

"What? What?" said Timothy and Sarah-Jane together.

Titus turned from the window and looked down at his cousins.

He said, "I think we found the lion. And I know we found the lamb."

14

The Lion and the Lamb

Naturally, Timothy and Sarah-Jane had to see for themselves.

Titus knew it wasn't that they didn't take his word for it. It was just too exciting not to see firsthand.

"It's a lamb all right," said Timothy.

"He's so sweet!" exclaimed Sarah-Jane. "He looks just like Alexander."

Titus knew what Sarah-Jane meant. The lamb certainly did seem to go with Alexander.

There was no car in the garage. The lamb snoozed peacefully on a shelf among some tools. The dolly stood nearby on the floor.

Titus was dying to see if Alexander was really under the burlap. He wanted to take him home and see what he looked like with the lamb curled up beside him.

Then suddenly Titus realized that Alexander would never again be tucked away in the corner of the attic as his own private lion. He belonged to the city and would have to go somewhere else—where everyone could see him. It was sad and exciting at the same time.

All of these thoughts went flying through Titus's mind in just a second. The real question was what to do now. Somehow it didn't seem right to sneak into the garage and take him back. They would have to get help.

Timothy was the fastest runner, so they decided he should go for the grown-ups.

"Whatever you do," said Titus. "Don't let them make you stop to explain! Just get them here on the double!"

Timothy took off like the wind, and Titus and Sarah-Jane stayed behind, standing guard.

Not that there was much they could do if someone came along and decided to take the lion and the lamb. Scream for help? Get the license plate number of the car? That was about it.

Sarah-Jane bounced from one foot to the other. Titus knew how she felt. It was *excru-*

ciating having to wait like this.

Suddenly Sarah-Jane gave a little scream. A car had turned into the alley.

It was headed right toward the garage.

15

Augustus Finch

*T*he car stopped and a man got out. Was this the thief? With his white hair and beard and twinkling blue eyes, he looked more like Santa Claus. The name on his cap said *Gus*.

Suddenly he spotted Titus and Sarah-Jane. "What are you kids doing here?" he asked.

Titus gulped and turned to look up the alley.

Where was Timothy?

He was right there. Just in the nick of time. With all four grown-ups hurrying along behind him.

"What's going on here?" asked Gus.

"I think we need to ask you the same question," said Titus's father a little breathlessly. "You see, we had a burglary at my aunt and uncle's this morning, and the children claim the missing item is in your garage."

"What? How?" said Gus.

"We followed the dolly tracks," said Sarah-Jane calmly. "You have to give them back, you know."

"What? Who?"

"The lion and the lamb," said Timothy.

"They belong to the city," said Titus. "The lion was in the attic for years and years. And the grown-ups didn't even know it, because they thought I made him up. But I didn't. I don't know where the lamb was. But he's in that garage now."

Gus looked as if he was about to protest. But then he sighed and said, "The lamb was in someone's garden all this time. I found him by accident only last month. I had been searching for years. Ever since the library was torn down and my sculpture disappeared."

"*Your* sculpture!" cried Timothy. He looked at the old man's hat. "*Gus,*" he read. "Is that short for—?"

"Augustus," said the man. "Augustus Finch at your service."

"The *artist!*" said Timothy in an awed voice.

Augustus Finch smiled. He said, "The guy who stole the lamb told me a pal of his took the lion. But he said this friend was too nervous to have it sitting out so he just stashed him in the attic. That just broke my heart. The guy I talked to had helped to carry the lion up there. So I knew exactly where they'd put it. I had my lamb back, and I was determined to get the lion back, too. I realized that the house was in this neighborhood, where my friend lives." He nodded toward the house that went with the garage.

Then he turned to Frank and Barbara. "I know I should have talked to you. But when I came over and saw you weren't home, I just took a chance and broke in. I was afraid you wouldn't admit to having the lion."

"We're not the ones who took him," said Granduncle Frank. "We didn't even know he was there. It must have been the people who owned the house before us. Don't worry. We won't press charges for the break-in. But we would like to see the lion and the lamb go back to the city. People are looking for them, you know."

Gus's face brightened at this news. "They are?"

"Yes," said Titus's mother, explaining about Lois and her committee. "Let's give her a call. She will positively *fly* over here to meet you."

Lois and several other committee members dropped everything and came rushing over to see the lion and the lamb.

Alexander has never looked better, Titus thought. It was decided that the lion and the lamb would have a place of honor at the new library.

Naturally the T.C.D.C. got a lot of fussing over for finding them.

Before the cousins left for home, they went back up to the attic for a quiet moment.

Titus went to the spot where Alexander had been for Titus's whole life. "I'm really going to miss my lion," he said.

"What lion?" asked Timothy with a perfectly straight face.

"That Titus!" said Sarah-Jane, shaking her head and smiling sweetly. "What an imagination!"

The End

Series for Young Readers*
From Bethany House Publishers

★ ★ ★

THE ADVENTURES OF CALLIE ANN
by Shannon Mason Leppard
Readers will giggle their way through the true-to-life escapades of Callie Ann Davies and her many North Carolina friends.

★ ★ ★

BACKPACK MYSTERIES
by Mary Carpenter Reid
This excitement-filled mystery series follows the mishaps and adventures of Steff and Paulie Larson as they strive to help often-eccentric relatives crack their toughest cases.

★ ★ ★

THE CUL-DE-SAC KIDS
by Beverly Lewis
Each story in this lighthearted series features the hilarious antics and predicaments of nine endearing boys and girls who live on Blossom Hill Lane.

★ ★ ★

RUBY SLIPPERS SCHOOL
by Stacy Towle Morgan
Join the fun as home-schoolers Hope and Annie Brown visit fascinating countries and meet inspiring Christians from around the world!

★ ★ ★

THREE COUSINS DETECTIVE CLUB®
by Elspeth Campbell Murphy
Famous detective cousins Timothy, Titus, and Sarah-Jane learn compelling Scripture-based truths while finding—and solving—intriguing mysteries.

* (ages 7–10)
9611